Man of Stories

Originally: 'A song under a rock'

a short play

Brittney Pilarcik

MAN OF STORIES

ACT ONE

Scene: A quiet country road, lined with trees and bushes. The sun is beginning to set, casting long shadows on the ground. RAZIM is standing near a crossroads, looking at a map or his phone with a frustrated expression. ELFIE is wandering around, occasionally looking at RAZIM with a mix of concern and amusement.

RAZIM

    (focused on his map, does not look up.)
  I'm busy Elfie,

ELFIE

    (throws his hands up in exasperation,
      walking over to RAZIM. Begins pacing)
Those are the two worst words put together. You can rather say you are not important to me. You're always busy! You're going to drive someone crazy one day—those are the only two words you know! I'm busy and I never tell anyone how busy I am, you should think about that! - Just take a walk with me, a nice stroll! Come on, we never do this anymore! I've been asking for weeks for you to go on a walk with me, - let's catch up like old times! When we were younger! We're getting to be old men now! You and I—I swear to God, could you look at me for five minutes!

RAZIM

    (Finally looks up from the map, sighs,
      and shakes his head.)
I have proper engagements, I'm meeting with

        people who can actually help me to succeed
        in life

ELFIE
        I get it, I do - you want a name for
        yourself, but come on!

RAZIM
        Do you know where we are?

ELFIE
        It was a left or a right at the fork of the
        road, I see I can't really remember now -

RAZIM
        (Throws the map down in frustration, takes
        a deep breath, and then composes
        himself.)

        I'm supposed to be dining tonight with
        important, successful people! I say, important
        and highly successful people - people who
        polish their shoes, calculate risks, iron
        their shirts, comb their hair every hour, wear
        rings, always save, never splurge on excess,
        grow beards, ride horses, do arithmetic for
        fun just to keep their minds sharp, wear lots
        of plaid and geometrical shapes, reflect on
        soviet art in their free time, drink alcohol
        only in the pleasure of friends or when in
        deep thought, people who know people who are
        willing to help me! The man in the city! The
        city that will give me the power and gold I
        deserve! Give me worth!

ELFIE

        (Nods slowly, then points in a random
        direction.) It must've been a left then, yes -
        yes I know - I care about you - and I don't

wear plaid! Or know math, or really all that
other stuff - especially the drinking part!
The other stuff, I mean who are these people!
I'm not so sure you should be making so much
of an effort, I mean do they even have time for
you?

RAZIM
    They are important people who can help me
    find status. Yes! They are exactly the
    kind of people I need in my life to live
    the life I want to live!

ELFIE
    Bet they don't know how to skin and
    deep fry a chicken though, do they?

RAZIM
    We're so lost, aren't we?

ELFIE
    I don't exactly see anyone out here
    playin' any pianos with a compass that
    says you are here!

RAZIM
    I should never ever have gone for a walk with
    you, look at where we are! There's nothing
    here! No signs, no posts nothing to tell us
    even which way we've been coming from

ELFIE
    We could probably start a new life out
    here, honestly, I think this is not so
    bad! Maybe even start our own city!

RAZIM
    Let's just keep walking this way! I believe
it might've been that way we were walking, oh no
 it's getting dark - I think this way, come on

                          Elfie!

ELFIE
     Oh my friend, don't worry we're going to be
     okay! Honestly, we really are! Things will
     work out - remember when we were kids!
     Everything always worked out for us in the
     end

RAZIM
     That's not exactly how I remember things

                    (A quiet country road, the sun now
                    lower in the sky, casting long
                    shadows. RAZIM and ELFIE
                    continue walking, the frustration and
                    weariness evident in their movements.)

ELFIE

                    (Walks ahead, gesturing expansively with his
                               arms as he talks.)

Soon we'll be making new homes for ourselves, can
you imagine being lost at sea - this kinda feels
like it - I love the sea! With all its might and
power under you, and the abyss of nothingness just
sitting there and you have no idea what or where you
are in the sea. The sea is so powerful, you know
when I was a kid, and I know you know this but I
used to chase jellyfish in the heat of August.
During the afternoons, I would chase them when I was
alone. I wasn't very bright, I know this, but
several times I got stung and once I was caught in
the drift of a current! It brought me out like a
hypnotizing wind that I just laid back in and felt
myself drifting, but it was so nice I couldn't get
out! But once I realized how far I was I had to
start swimming back, I almost drowned! Luckily your
body pushes you to fight to live otherwise I

thought, this isn't such a bad way to go! My mind
said, let the sea take me! But my body, and I was
in better shape then - but the body said fight! Had
it not been for a friendly seaman out taking a last
look right before heading home, he is the one who
caught me! Took me back to shore and said, 'son you
better not be out there chasing jellyfish anymore,
no one's gonna save you next time!' I said, 'sir,' -
and I really said this - I said, 'sir, I will never
forget this day' and I never forgot it! Imagine if
he saw me here, in this forest now talking to you
about that day! (chuckles) I never told him I went
days after that doing the same thing, I think I got
addicted to the adrenaline! Or maybe the sea, or
maybe the peacefulness of a tremendous amount of
uncertainty all around you, but you can see it.
That's the difference in life I think, in life you
have uncertainties and abysses full of dangerous
creatures but you don't see them like you do in the
sea

RAZIM

        (Groans and rolls his eyes.)
    For godsakes, I forgot how much you like to
    talk - it's been hours we are out here
    already

ELFIE
        (shrugs) That's true and we have come a long
way now

RAZIM
        (looks around, worry creeping into his voice)
    We may have to sleep out here, can you
    believe it! All the important people of the
    city will be wondering where I am! Eating
    their fancy cheeses and with all those
    spoons, laughing about how great life is in a
    great big house with a garden! And I'm out

here in the wilderness with you! Elfie, we
have got to find a way back soon

ELFIE
Do you hear someone playing the violin?

RAZIM
What? Um, actually I think I do

ELFIE
A good sign that must be

RAZIM
An excellent sign! A person must be

out there!

ELFIE

   (Starts walking briskly towards the sound,
          animated and excited.)
   What sort of music do you think he's playing?
   An opera? A solo? No, a duet made for a piano
   and a violin! I do believe it sounds like a
   symphony, a powerful symphony which hasn't
   begun yet because so far there is only one
   musician playing! But soon, my dear friend, I
   believe there will be more musicians, more
   instruments! And we will sit back and listen
   tonight and enjoy the notes of every one of
   them hitting the notes again and again while
   we gaze at the stars! We don't have any
   musicians who can play very well in the city
   where no one writes, dreams or plays anymore!
   They must've all come out here, to the forest!
   We could become our own musicians, don't you
   think! Don't you think we have the power to do
   that! Make our own music, tie those banana
   trees leaves together and make our own songs!
   Look what we could do with the branches! Turn
   them into sticks and bows! We could make our
   own orchestra out here!

RAZIM
     Enough Elfie, really - I'm tired of listening
     to you jabber all the time! You're foolish
     thinking like this!

ELFIE
     Like what!

RAZIM
     I think we will just be lost forever.

ELFIE

     No way! we will find our way by looking at the
     stars, by listening to the sounds of the waves
     telling us which way to go - against the
     currents! We will be found one day, for sure -
     and they will paint us as modern-day pioneers,
     once lost men in the humdrum of the mundane
     boring life of competition with fellow men, but
     who are now the envy of the world, of every
     man and woman stuck in a routine of life, look
     you see there - look at that bird, is it
     friend or foe? No one ever cares to ask but in
     the jungles of the city only people want what
     they can get out of you. You see, even though
     we are lost, deserted, and alone - we have the
     greatest adventures any modern-day man could
     ever wish for himself! We have it all! the
     guts, the dreams! the imagination! the sea and
     all her power beckoning us out to adventures
     we couldn't even dream of! Why do you sit
     there thinking of everything you lost when, in
     fact, you have gained so much here. It's better
     to have the imagination of a child, than the
     reality of the world because in the end you are
     the reality creating the world! I think that
     much anyway. I want to hear music! I want to be
     a musician. I want to dance, let's dance! Let's

        dance on this sand and on this shore, and
        let's hop like kangaroos.

        ELFIE begins to dance playfully, trying to
        lighten the mood. RAZIM watches, a mix of
        frustration and reluctant amusement on his face.

RAZIM
        (wiping sweat from his brow, agitated) You
        can't dance and hop like a kangaroo when
        there's food to be caught! If you don't catch
        the food and if you don't think of the
        consequences, you will be left here. You can't
        all-day play music. It's just .. it doesn't
        work like that. We're going to be hungry and we
        are driving ourselves crazy standing in this
        heat. It's better for us to make a bit of
        shade and to rest so we don't over-exert our
        bodies.

ELFIE
        (crosses arms defiantly) Wrong!

RAZIM
        (exasperated) What?

ELFIE
        Wrong wrong wrong

RAZIM
        I'm not wrong, you're wrong

ELFIE
        No You

RAZIM
        What?

 ELFIE
        You are wrong! I do say. Hey, what's that -
    do you see that in the distance? what is it?

RAZIM
     I don't see anything!

ELFIE
     Look, it's right there, come here where I
     stand you can see it better

RAZIM
     (moves to Elfie, squinting) Where?

ELFIE
     (pointing emphatically) Look at where I'm
     pointing, do you see it now?

RAZIM
     No what is it? (shaking his head,

confused)

ELFIE
     It's a Lure

RAZIM
     Oh my god. Elfie, your imagination, it's
     killing me. Okay, enlighten me - what's a
     lure

ELFIE
     You don't know what a Lure is?

RAZIM
     (sighs heavily) No, please... if you must,
     explain to me what you've come up with

          ELFIE
               (speaking with dramatic flair)

     A lure is something big, hairy, and ugly - but
never mind the appearances - a lure is something so
captivating in its.... oddities that you can't help
 but to be drawn to it. When you see it - it's like
               you can't stop looking!

you have to stare and stare until you can't
stop! And then, when you realize what's
happened you're too overcome by its embrace
that you are forever cluched by it's wormy
slimy little arms that I believe it has, and
I'm sure the color is purple or something like
that !

RAZIM
        (Sarcastically, throwing hands in
  the air.) Then maybe you shouldn't be
                  looking

ELFIE
     I can't help it as I said - it's captivating
me!

RAZIM

     Well, stop it you clown of man! I
     mean, your imagination - it's just

ELFIE
     I can't!

RAZIM

  (Grabs ELFIE's shoulders, shaking him gently)
     Stop, I said stop looking!

ELFIE

  (Pushes RAZIM's hands away, stepping back)
     Let's go to it!

RAZIM
         No, come on listen to yourself - you will
never be able to get rid of what you have just
                      said -

ELFIE
       Of what? what did I say?

RAZIM
       You idiot! You know what go, just go to that
       creature you see.

ELFIE
       I am! Maybe I'll get a warm hug out of it. I
will go to find out! Goodbye Razim.

RAZIM

              (Throws his hands up in frustration,
               turns away, then turns back, yelling.)
       Uff, well and go - just go already. Better to
       not have you and be alone than to be here
       listening to you jabbing like a dingleberry
       politician - why couldn't I be stuck here with
       a mime for crying out loud. Damn it. Hey Hey!
       Come back, come back!! Come back - don't go,
       I'm sorry for what I said, ... Come back!!!!

              (ELFIE disappears into the forest.
              RAZIM stands alone, the weight of the
              situation finally
              sinking in. He takes a deep breath and
              starts walking in the direction ELFIE
              went, muttering to himself.)

              (Navigating through the thick
                          underbrush,

        grumbling)
Nettles, and trees and bush and nothing nice of
here or there with all this crap - the
emptiness of solitude of a life not worth
living, what the hell did I do to deserve such
a life of this. Could've been with my red
carpet friends, laughing and discussing
politics, the subject of important people
talking about shooting eagles in the sky while
also talking about being, eco friendly - !
Hey! Hey ! god, what an idiot, can't hear a
goddamn thing - what the hell, who's there?
hello? Hey! come here,

CONTINUES WANDERING THROUGH THE FOREST

ELFIE

        (From a distance, slightly panicked)
Razim I seem to have lost my way over here
do you - think there's any way you could
help me.

RAZIM

        (Rolls his eyes, sighs heavily)
If you weren't the only man on this godforsaken
land,   - but since you happen to be my only
friend here what are the chances. . . give me
your hand,

ELFIE
     (Appearing through the trees, reaching out.)
     Do you know where we are?

RAZIM
     We are lost

ELFIE
     We've always been lost,

RAZIM
     Even more lost now.

ELFIE
     Perhaps we've made a great actual discovery
     from this - Have you seen those tall trees
     beaming over us, shall we climb one of them?

 RAZIM
     Absolutely not! That's too dangerous and if
we fall - we'll have no doctors around to help us.

ELFIE
     In that case, we should - climb high and far.
     You know once when I was a child, I believed
     I could fly - almost did once but the
     neighbor had to come and get me down when he
     saw I had my feet stuck in a branch, but
     otherwise - I could've done it, could've made
     a spectacle about it too

RAZIM
     We must not talk like fools

ELFIE
     I'm not a fool, I'm an intellectual, and as an
     intellectual, I must say we should climb that
     tree! Perhaps, we'll have a mishap or two, but
     nothing more than a nap will recover us from
     the troubles and we'll have the time of our
     lives racking on and on how our lives were
     forever -

RAZIM
     Is there really not a single person out here
     that can help us!

ELFIE
     (Suddenly alert, tilting his head to listen.)
     Do you hear that?

RAZIM
     (Sarcastically, rolling his eyes.) A man,
     losing his status, privilege, and honour as
     we speak. Yes, I hear my future dwindling
     down to embers

ELFIE
     (Excitedly, pointing into the distance.) No
     no, I hear someone playing the violin!

RAZIM
     (Groaning, throwing his hands up.) Not this
   again Elfie! Really, come on we are gonna die
                         here!

     ELFIE
          Listen! Listen carefully as if your pitiful
     sorrowful dreams weren't being murdered as we
                          speak!

RAZIM
     Thanks, Elfie

ELFIE
     Listen, really listen

RAZIM
     (Realizing.) Oh yeah, I do hear a violin

   ELFIE
          Look over on that hill there's a man or at
     least a silhouette of a man! Should we go to
                          him?

RAZIM
(Concerned, looking towards the figure.A
stranger in the woods) yes - yes we have no
other option but to go to him Elfie what else
are we going to do here! Plus it looks like a
storm may be approaching, maybe we can find
some shelter with him.

ELFIE
Have you ever thought that Chinese food always
tastes better when you're not in China

RAZIM
(puzzled) You've never been to China, so how
would -

ELFIE
(interrupting with a grin) It's just what
I've heard

RAZIM
Elfie, please - I beg you - stop talking! I'm
hungry, I'm tired, I don't want to be here
with you out here another minute more!

ELFIE
(playful) I'm your best friend and you know
it!

RAZIM
You are not, you are not my friend - you are
going to be an annoying memory after this - we grew
up together that's it. What in the world is this
guy doing up there?

ELFIE
(calling out as he cheerfully approaches)

Excuse me sir! Excuse me, sir - uhm, hello -
oh what should I say to a man in a top hat,
you really have dressed up today! For an
audience of no one

MAN OF STORIES
        (with a flourish) Eh moi? Eh, what are
        you doing here? And no one can ever
        overdress

RAZIM
        (assertive, taking charge) No, we ask the
        questions here, let's get to the point, what
        are you doing here - why are you here and how
        the heck do we get out of here!

MAN OF STORIES
        (nonchalantly) I suppose that eh, depends
        then - doesn't it?

ELFIE
        Depends on what

RAZIM
        (cutting in, determined) No, we are not going
        into this sort of conversation, we are getting
        out of here - sir, please, please look at me
        and tell me where we are and how to get out

MAN OF STORIES
        (intriguingly) What is it that you seek?

RAZIM
        We're lost, we are looking to go back to the
        city from whence we came on this
        unbelievable journey, ill-prepared we've
        come and I've let this fool lead me! Please,
        just tell me how to go back

MAN OF STORIES
        (curiously) The city you say - interesting,

ELFIE
     It's like a different type of wilderness
     there, honestly could take your time in
     giving us the directions really

RAZIM
     Elfie, not now - okay - please, look we live
there

MAN OF STORIES
     (philosophically) But what is it that you seek,
     you live - but you seek as well - everyone
     seeks something! Twice in my life have I seen
     men who do not seek and even they in the end
     with their last gasp for air and as they held
     onto what last minutes they had, they told me
     had they but found a purpose to seek then they
     may have passed on with a twinkle in their
     eye. Everyone desires, yearns for something.
     It's the purpose of all stories, of all
     characters and of all men. Men die for honour,
     men die for desire in seeking that which they
     believe to be their purpose, what gives them
     meaning - to see others look at them on their
     higher ground, on their higher path. Love and
     to be loved, people look for purpose in all
     sorts of things, in objects, in diety and in
     relationships - but they are all seeking it!

ELFIE
     Even me?

MAN OF STORIES
     What do the deer and man have in common,
     wobbly legs and both are being hunted - one
     by man one by god. Tell me, what do you yearn
     for?

RAZIM
    (urgently) If I tell you what I seek will you
    tell me how to get out of here

ELFIE
    (tripping over a root, laughing) Uf, I tripped!
    Silly me

MAN OF STORIES
    When you can't see where to go where do you go?
    When you don't know what to do, what do you
    do? What do you do when in solitude and in
    vain you cry out and say someone help me!
    (plays with his trinkets) If you tell me what
    keeps you up at night, what makes your heart
    excited, and the purpose that makes you a man
    in this life - I will give it to you and of
    course lead you out of this dark wilderness you
    seem to despise so much

ELFIE
    It's really not that bad out here, honestly, I
    kinda like the solitude

MAN OF STORIES
    (turning to Razim, intrigued) You know what
    men seek in the city

RAZIM
    Fortune.

ELFIE
    Oh, I was going to say that too!

MAN OF STORIES
    (probing) And this fortune, is it something
    that keeps you up at night, motivates you at
    dawn - sits in the distance taunting you and
    do you at times wish it upon yourself to attain
    - a sole man on a journey to find his fortune.

                Does it occupy your thoughts and tell you above
                all else, your worth in this life?

RAZIM
                I suppose it does

MAN OF STORIES
                (a riddle in his tone) A thistle here a
                memory there - but where do they all go?

ELFIE
                (eagerly) To the forest!

MAN OF STORIES
                Nope!

ELFIE
                To the -

MAN OF STORIES
                Nope! (enjoying and whimsically behaving)

ELFIE
                Where do they go! Oh please tell me!

MAN OF STORIES
                To the home made with lavender

RAZIM
                Elfie, he's playing games with you, okay
                enough riddles! No word games, no plays

MAN OF STORIES
                Your wish granted, your heart never satisfied.

RAZIM
                My heart is barely holding, no oil or riddle
                can fix that

MAN OF STORIES
                I knew a man once, who believed in goodness,
                he was kind and warm, you know the man. Once
                I met this man,

eager was I in his confidence. These kinds of
humans, well they just walk into the room and
you find yourself at ease with a man like
that. I said to him, you seem to have it all. I
do, said the man - I said, and is there
anything you are seeking, something that you
want? What gets your feet moving in the
morning, and you know what a man like a god
said to me? He said: 'More!' Never satisfied,
this happens to them, always wanting never
satisfied - these are the traits of the man. He
got his fortune because he came to me -
seeking, I said I know where fortune lies - you
see, I may be a myth in your stories but I
also have a degree in economics, spending time
in the forest, you get bored ! I said, I have
the answer for your fortune, but because I love
a good story, no fortune I give without a
threat - the one I give to you today holds
blind men and creatures in your future, oh and
much darkness in your ending! To men you see
the fortune they seek never allows both
happiness and pleasure. The man went mad, left
the living souls around him who cared for him
and hid behind his gold singing songs and
telling the air around him what he did to get
his fortune. The entire village tell stories of
his madness and look on him with pity now as he
sits with a face (cynically) he in torment
tried to peel off with his hands! He turned to
a beast you see, a laughing joke for all who
know him. In pity he cried out! In vain no one

answered. He said, is this what becomes of me - after all I did! An oak tree of a man he was brought to a twig of a spoiled shrub. Another man sold his wife and children for a bit of the life made of gold. I found his family in a cave one day and as I was passing by I asked them what happened to them, they told me the story of the man who gave up everything just to have a bit of power in this life, they grew ill in the cave and I went to the man in the city who was dining with royals and politicians all dressed in fine clothes and eating from silver plates, and I said do you know what happened to your family, I said this when he was alone away from jealous ears, I said your family, do you know what has happened to them, and I explained. He said I can not leave my status of gleaning eyes and abundant feasts nor my seat next to people who actually matter in this life - I said, I am a Man of Stories, I said, I will give you a story - he of course, did not want to hear what a man like me has to say, I said listen very carefully because my stories change the path of men. I said, a man like you shall continue to live in the embrace of women and strangers of position and power, but for you I know your story, your advisor will betray you for nothing more than a stick of butter, - butter was very valuable then at that time, you see - he will then take everything you have and your name will disappear from the earth. These kinds of men will always continue it's in their hearts - there's nothing you can do - soon he began to lose feeling, touch in his skin. I said, go back to your family before you lose your touch forever. But it was too late. His friend had already betrayed him.

ELFIE
     Excuse me, I don't mean to interrupt I would
     however say that that's terrible , what sad
     stories - really truly sad, but I just have
     to know - are you like a ghost, or something?

MAN OF STORIES
     I'm a Man of Stories

ELFIE
     Hm, nice so you're a man right? I mean your
     skin does look

MAN OF STORIES
     I am a man, why are you even asking me?

RAZIM
     Elfie, come on have some respect for this
stranger

MAN OF STORIES
     I feel like it's pretty obvious, I'm a man?
     What kind of? Of course -

ELFIE
     I don't know, in the city I suppose you can
     never be too sure. Gee that was a hard story
     to listen to - don't you have something -
     like perky?

MAN OF STORIES
     As I was saying, I'm a man - a man of
     many manly features - I mean, I'm
     wearing a suit! I have a beard!

RAZIM
     Ignore him, really he doesn't know better -

MAN OF STORIES
     What even was I saying!

RAZIM
     Fortune! I want it all, I want everything I can
     get - I want the life of riches - to feel like
     I belong! To have men gaze at me, to have -

ELFIE
     I gaze at you Razim!

RAZIM
     Men who matter! Men who do important work, who
     dress in fine clothes - who say things like
     EBITA and GDP and words that mean important
     things, like market and stock and forging
     ahead! or interest rates! These are men who
     matter!

MAN OF STORIES
     Do you know of the stories of the men who
     have come to this forest and found a
     fortune?

ELFIE
     We do! Thought they were myths but yes! Are you
going to help us!

RAZIM
     I would do anything for a fortune

MAN OF STORIES
     The wind blows for everyone, doesn't it - but
     it does not blow for me for it never reaches my
     skin - I'm a man of many fortunes, a man who
     knows where fortunes lie. I help men find
     their fortune here in this world. In the dark
     and in the shadows, behind the bushes in the
     night, under the night sky just around the
     corner and up the hill to the place I've
     marked, lies a song under a rock. Sweet and
     delicate in the beginning of the melody with
     small chords to make you wonder, gradually

getting stronger, increased in tempo and
running like notes on a page. I've hidden it
you see!

RAZIM
     What?

MAN OF STORIES
     A melody is such a light thing, such a
     beautiful thing, a thing - I cannot name. A
     melody is such an enormous gift, a beautiful
     gift a sweet gift. What a reward what a hopeful
     gift - what a great rewarding gift - such an
     enormous gift. A melody is such a strange
     obsession, truly a strange obsession, what a
     mystifying obsession something which invades
     the mind. Truly what an enormous obsession. A
     melody is such a curse, a terrible curse - a
     creature really - really sticks to you and
     doesn't let go. So addicting is a melody -
     such a thing to behold a wonderful beautiful
     curse, can't describe it really. Just that's
     how it is. I wrote one down a melody you see,
     a key to a fortune I have hidden in this world.

RAZIM
     And you would just give us a fortune then? If
we hear the melody?

MAN OF STORIES
     Hearts of man, spin the wheel - tell me more
     stories of the lives of mankind. Of women and
     of man, of man I call them - all who walk
     under the sun. Everyone! - you see, all you
     know - anyone that has ever come from the
     womb has a story to tell - a purpose they
     seek, something that wakes them up in the
     morning. I love to see what a man would do
     for gold. Call it my obsession.

RAZIM
          And how are we to know that you are telling
          the truth. You are just a man in the
          forest after all.

MAN OF STORIES
          But you have heard the stories of me, right?
          In the city they do talk of me don't they?

ELFIE
          Oh yes it's true! I have heard of you -
          Razim, I believe he's telling the truth! How
          lucky are we to have gone on this walk
          together!

RAZIM
          True, yes. But all the same. How do we know you
          speak truth.

MAN OF STORIES
          Maybe I do - maybe I don't - but what you seek
          is what interests me the most. I tell you now
          all that I am. I want more than anything, a
          story to tell. I want to see what drives men
          mad - what makes them go to war, leave their
          home, marry and cheat, why they go mad, why in
          toil they find pride! You see, I'm interested
          in man. You are man, I want to know, what will
          you do for a fortune.

ELFIE
          This is just - so much fun. I am in! I love
          stories too!

RAZIM
          Elfie, please. Be logical. This is just...
          Okay, look - you know the way out - show us
          the way out, give us the fortune - la , la ,
          la we will do it. Okay, I agree. I want the
          fortune, take us out and we will do it.

MAN OF STORIES
        The tree said to the ground what the fox said
        to the bird what the squirrel said to the
        chord that changes season of producing and
        giving and of taking and destroying the chord
        you must find two things you must find people
        who give you a song and the instruments to play
        them with -

RAZIM
        God I hate riddles and fantastical obsessions
        and ridiculous nonsense - oh yeah, let me
        guess - there's a genie in a carpet or a
        talking sock with six little pandas living in
        it speaking in Greek?

MAN OF STORIES
        Do you speak Greek!

RAZIM
        No! Of course not!

  ELFIE
        He's always doing this to me! Surprises me,
         gets my hopes up and then boom - just
                      disappointment

MAN OF STORIES
        The two of you are friends? Right?

RAZIM
        Oh, we grew up together

ELFIE
        We're best friends

MAN OF STORIES
        What does everyone truly desire? Yearn
         for? Go to great lengths for?

RAZIM
        Fortune

MAN OF STORIES
     And what else -

ELFIE
     To love - and to be loved

MAN OF STORIES
     People look for purpose in all sorts of
     things , in objects - in relationships - but
     it is in them and that's what the chord does
     - It makes you stop and hopefully wonder
     what is your purpose - gives you greatness -
     If you follow me, I will take you to a
     fortune made for men. It's up here, come I'll
     take you

RAZIM
     What, no absolutely not -

ELFIE
     We have no other choice Razim, we really
     have no other choice, we don't know
     where we are! Come on

                  THEY CONTINUE UP A PATH

MAN OF STORIES
     Tonight I am going to give you a melody! The
     key to your fortune! You have chosen, under
     this rock, a song - a melody you can never
     unhear. A fortune it will reward you with. But
     before you receive the fortune you must agree
     to find me stories in the city of men and women
     who seek, find what they seek and bring me
     their answers. Only after will the melody give
     you the fortune. I made the melody you see, I'm
     quite proud of it. It will lead you and guide
     you, and tell you where to go and calm your
     anxious minds. But it will also in time unlock

          your greatest desires!

     ELFIE
              Yes! That's what we want! A song under a
     rock! That is mine, something special! Something
      to make us special Razim! This is the best day
                             ever!

RAZIM
          You are a fool, no this is insane, do not
          lift up that rock

     ELFIE
              Lift it! By the way, do these men, the ones
      who get the fortune do they have happy endings

MAN OF STORIES
          It is up to them to decide

ELFIE
          I'm so ready, lift it! I'm ready!

MAN OF STORIES
          You will have to go into the city - the road
          will be lit after I lift this rock. I am like
          this, someone curious of the songs of man - of
          the pursuit of every living person. This is my
          reward, for giving you this melody - the key
          to a new adventure make sure to bring me many
          stories. (lifts the rock)

  A SONG BEGINS TO PLAY AS THE MAN OF STORIES

DISAPPEARS

                          ACT TWO

ELFIE
Did you see the way he just disappeare

RAZIM
God I hate magic

ELFIE
I don't think that was magic

RAZIM
So what was that then?

ELFIE
Spiritual

RAZIM
It can't be spiritual, most likely it was just
a man in a goofy costume and he has fooled us.
This is what we're going to do, we're going
back somehow! I have a ton of work to do you
have no idea! I got so much work, I'm a very
busy man you know this - I am very busy and I
have a ton of work on real projects which
brings in real success, not this mystical,
whimsical, rubbish dinner made for fools we've
just been fed. I then have a ton of meetings
to attend. Probably catered as well, and
definitely full of big big tables with lots of
presentations! Things you don't understand
Elfie.

ELFIE
But what if it is true, what if there really is
a fortune, we could be like Bonnie and Clyde -
the pair of us!

RAZIM

What! No, Bonnie and Clyde were bank
robbers! Criminals, they were insane with
a terrible ending!

ELFIE

Okay, bad example geez, let me think - Harry
Potter and Hermoine

RAZIM

Absolutely not! They were, geez Elfie, they
were no - no no!

ELFIE

Frodo and Sam!

RAZIM

No! Well, if we were I'd be Frodo though, but
no ! No no no!

ELFIE

Timon and Pumbaa!

RAZIM

Enough, Elfie - No, we are going back in our
separate ways! How about this, if he is
telling the truth there will be another sign,
right? Surely if this melody is how we are to
find a fortune then we'll be given
confirmation and not by birds or stars or some
gnome in the forest or some random tree talking
about some legendary nonsense really - I don't
have time for this at all

ELFIE

Well, it's not like we're going to get an excel
spreadsheet saying this is what the man in the
forest says to do, and this is how to get all
the women you want in the world. You know, if I
were rich I definitely would get fat

RAZIM
        You already are. This is just absolutely crazy
        - why am I having this conversation with you.
        Let's just go back

ELFIE
        Look, there's a man in the distance

RAZIM
        Let's go to him and pray he'ssane

    THEY BEGIN WALKING TOWARDS A MAN IN THE SHADOWS

RAZIM
        Excuse me, we've gotten ourselves a bit lost
        and we are unsure of our steps and whether or
        not we are on the path that leads to

ELFIE
        to fortune!

RAZIM
        To the city, shh

ELFIE
        We met a man with a top hat!

RAZIM
        Shh!

ELFIE
        Told us we could find a fortune!

RAZIM
        Be quiet

ELFIE
        Gave us a melody!

RAZIM
        Are you serious right now, never knows when
        silence is more powerful than words - see
        Elfie, this is something you need to learn

                    FARMER
          Ah yes, the Man of Stories he calls
     himself, yes I know him, creepy looking dude,
                    possibly French

ELFIE
     Creepy

RAZIM
     Totally weird

FARMER
          Anyways

ELFIE
          Anyways, so what's his deal?

RAZIM
          Is he crazy?

FARMER
          Most likely, however, he is known for his
          stories because they do come to be - he is
          known in the lands for this. Sure makes
          storytelling a bit of fun I suppose. He does
          also work for an extremely powerful,
          influential and incredibly important family who
          always polish their shoes, always wear designer
          clothes, and eat molded cheese while discussing
          politics with cigars in a big big house - but
          he took it upon himself to be the teller of
          stories. I know he is a bit strange, but if
          you've been visited by the Man of Stories he is
          sure to do everything in his power to tell a
          tale of destiny for those who are desperate for
          something. He finds your desperation, reveals
          it and then puts you on some sort of a spell
          or path if you will that leads you to what you
          want. Quite boring really. I think he just
          likes telling stories and wants to learn more
          about us humans. Weirdo really. Has nothing
          better to do but pretend to be living in some

          fairytale.

ELFIE
     This must be destiny, it really must be! Our
     destiny - aren't you excited!

               THEY KEEP WALKING

RAZIM
     Elfie, this is insane - I mean, let's use our
     heads right now and be practical - do you
     really believe this

ELFIE
     Look, there he is again! What a creepy
     looking man, but very stylish

MAN OF STORIES
     You are questioning my fortune is that

not true?

RAZIM
     What are you, god? Man, give me a break

MAN OF STORIES
     Before your feet step towards the path which
     will lead you to the city, you must be aware
     that you are both now carrying my melody which
     if fulfilled will give you a fortune. If you do
     nothing with my melody then I will come and
     destroy you - I'm kidding hah, I really am
     kidding.

ELFIE
     ha, what a joke - uhm, really funny right
     Razim? You are really a man of theatrics

MAN OF STORIES
     I do love the theater, anyways - please - find
     in the city men and women who are seeking -
     ask them what it is they seek - tell them to
     sing you a song, I am curious! You see, very
     curious of the songs of man - make sure you
     record them, tell them you are looking for a
     new melody, I love melodies! I really do, when
     you come back to me tell me of the songs of man
     and what it is they seek. Tell me and I will
     allow the song from under a rock to be the key
     to your fortune. Each of you, fortune for two.

RAZIM
     Yes - yes we get it - be gone already!

MAN OF STORIES
     You must find the chords and the instruments
     in the city, songs and melodies - the
     pursuit of man, my obsession

          MAN OF STORIES DISAPPEARS

ELFIE
     What now, what do we do? How do we even begin?

 RAZIM
      I have got no clue and to be honest, I am not
   sure I care what some crackhead in the forest
 says, he's a creep. Look, I went with you, I went
 for a walk with you, I lost my valuable time I'm
                  going to work.

ELFIE
     But you can't!

  RAZIM
        Yes, yes I can. Elfie, you can't just sit
  around listening to wackos and believing them,
 okay, I hate to break it to you like this but you

really need to become more self-aware. Ok? Think
for yourself, be a man. Come on, don't cry, look
 it's going to be okay, come on - stop - stop it
really! Elfie! what are you doing! Stop, please.
          I'll deal with this later.

ELFIE AND RAZIM PART WAYS, AND RAZIM GOES TO WORK.

COWORKER
     (comes up to RAZIM while he's walking) You have
     disappeared and been replaced in every single
     possible way, while you were gone I found new
     people to eat cheese with and to go to the
     indie cinema with, to discuss new theories and
     philosophies with while drinking very expensive
     water and there have been at least 6 new
     philosophers discovered with revelations that
     are way beyond your time and your knowledge to
     ever possibly understand. You've missed all the
     new subscriptions to the top magazines that
     everyone must read, as well as all the trending
     news, best shows and new styles. Your clothes
     are practically from a different century now
     and no one breathes every minute now - that's
     so old-fashioned, you must take a breath every
     5 to 6 minutes for you to be here.

RAZIM
     That's impossible!

COWORKER
     (holding his breath) I don't have time for
     this, you know I'm an incredibly busy person
     with time for people only with shined shoes,
     people who know people who know people who know
     people - who play at least one instrument and
     speak a minimum of five languages - I can't be
     bothered

BOSS
(also comes up after) You have lost your job,
   your position, your status and your shoes.

RAZIM
This is a joke, I haven't been gone that long!

BOSS
That's how it works, it works like this give me
your shoes. You should know this. I don't want to
   elaborate, but someone better looking, more
     charismatic, charming, much much smarter came
     in and I just couldn't say no, he must be
     important because he smiles and everyone just,
     well - he wins! That's what he does he's a
     winner, not you. It's the city. That's how it
     works here. Come on, give me your shoes. Hey,
     I'm sure you can look for another place where
     you can look out at tall building windows and
     see the sunset while drinking a glass of
     champagne and watching very important numbers
     go up and making calls to a man named Steve
     who does very very important work for the city

RAZIM
All I did was get a little lost and distracted
   for a few days! How could you let me, how could
   you let this happen! When will I ever be able to
   see another big stack of documents come by that
                only I can see!

BOSS
You'll figure it out, it's a fox eats rabbit
     kinda world

RAZIM
You mean dog eat dog

BOSS
That's the city we change expressions all the

time, keep up - lingo, linguistics, you should
learn something sometime! Anyways, you're
wasting my time, I gotta run with my whiskey
while I wave my hands and hold my breath
because now that's the trend of the day! - I
have important meetings to attend with
successful people who wake up extremely early
with large activities and lots and lots of data
and global initiatives to start. I can't be
wasting my time with you anymore

RAZIM TAKES OFF HIS SHOES AND GOES TO THE STREET

RAZIM
       Elfie! Elfie where are you! Oh, god where did
he go! Elfie! Where are you! I don't have a phone
anymore! Excuse me, have you seen my friend? He's
short and quite frankly needs to go on a more
nutrient-high diet because he's grown a bit around
the waist over the years, he's balding severely and
has a round face, he's usually smiling and humming!
He's my friend! He's kind, and usually wears baggy
pants! Have you seen him? Has anyone seen him? It
is incredibly important! It's a matter of life and
death! I must find him! He loves to watch the
godfather! He's overly talkative and always
blabbing, a bit annoying, slanted in the left eye,
a beard that won't grow! My friend, Elfie!

PERSON
       I can't say that your description describes
       anyone I've seen however it does seem like an
       interesting person, I hope you find him. By
       the way, could it be the bus driver for route
       204? He is friendly, jolly, balding, always
       kind, a bit slow but always on time with the
       busses and could use a more nutrient-based
       diet!

RAZIM
    Yes! I did forget to mention he drives a bus,
    but I'm unsure of the number

PERSON 2
    Definitely 204, he never shuts up! Always
    talking, I mean always talking!

RAZIM
    That must be him! He's my friend, where is he?

PERSON
    I told you, I don't know and I'm
    incredibly busy. This is the city you
    know, we don't have time for people
    unless they -

RAZIM
    I know, I know - are important ! He must be
    on that bus! I must find him! Elfie where
    were you! I was searching everywhere for
    you!

ELFIE
    So you believe!

RAZIM
    I don't believe in anything Elfie, but I have
    nothing else to do - I've just lost my job!

ELFIE
    Great!

RAZIM
    Not great Elfie! Terrible, what am I going to
do!

ELFIE
    We could go collect the stories from people -
and do the melody thing you know, from the guy in
the forest

RAZIM
     Elfie no absolutely not

ELFIE
     Just a suggestion.

RAZIM
     Okay. No, we should do it - I need the
     distraction. How do we begin?

ELFIE
     I suppose we just start asking people

RAZIM
     How

ELFIE
     Um. Like this I guess. (looks for a person)
     Excuse me, we're looking for what people seek
     - what makes them who they are - a story
     perhaps of every living being. A man in the
     forest wants to know

RAZIM
     Elfie - you can't say that!

ELFIE
     It is true though

SHOSHANA
     Me? I'm just a simple woman in this city
     I'm often unseen by the many eyes that
     pass by -

ELFIE
     Perfect!

SHOSHANA
     Oh

ELFIE
     See, we are looking for people with a story!
     You must have one!

RAZIM
Elfie, you can't just ask people like this

SHOSHANA
     Well, I'm a commoner you see - someone just
     common, ordinary really.

ELFIE
That's great! Us too really! You see, you must
have a story - everyone has one! You want to perhaps
share with us! A man in the forest he wants us to
collect stories, gave us a melody - says he wants
more stories to make a new song out of

RAZIM
Elfie no no - I'm sorry please don't listen to
us

SHOSHANA
     Well, I do have a story.

ELFIE
Tell us please!

SHOSHANA
     (pauses to think) Once I fell in love with a
     man, he was neither wealthy nor poor but made a
     humble home he spoke rarely and gave to the
     poor, he was neither dishonest nor greedy
     always left enough to share. But nothing is as
     good as an embrace. A lovely memory and a
     comfortable home. He enjoyed the time away more
     than the time together. I bought lilies for
     myself, to make me happy. I said to myself
     this will make the time full. I made myself
     pretty, I looked nice, I tried to smile even
     when it hurt - when he told me of all the
     people he met while I was at home. I took a
     pin and put it in my hair, I made it from
     things around the house. I said this is nice,
     begged for attention. I started to become very

lonely. Noises began to bother me. I'm
constantly trying to drown the sound out around
me. The sound of keys hitting. The sound of
water dropping. The sound of dry leaves hitting
the window. The sounds I don't like to hear. I
soon decided instead of waiting I would wander.
I like to wander you see I lost my confidence a
while ago and now I just wander. I left the
empty home, no one noticed not even my bed. I
asked everyone, what do I do with this
solitude? People told me go back home and wait,
be safe and look nice. Be like a lily and he
will return. Now I don't wait anymore. I do
things that make me happy. I buy my own
flowers, I make my days pass by with gentle
care. When you find the song will you remember
to play it for me. I wish I could help you I
really do , but tis so sweet to know noble men
are here looking to save us walking around with
no melody, no music, no love

ELFIE
        uh, yes - absolutely - what a nice um, story,
truly -

RAZIM
        Thank you for sharing ma'am. I wish,
        there was something we could say to
        you, but I'm afraid we don't know what
        to say. I have never heard such a - um,
        a tale

SHOSHANA

        (begins humming)

ELFIE
        Story

RAZIM
        Was that a story?

ELFIE
        Yeah, I think parts of it were

SHOSHANA
        It's alright. You have a story. (hums and walks
        away)

RAZIM
        Come on Elfie

                              THEY GO TO THE BAR

ELFIE
        Did you hear what she said? She called us

noble!

RAZIM
        Pass me some more - I'm not sure that was a

story

WAITER
        Do u have 20 cents I'm trying to raise money
        for some socks these ones hurt my feet

RAZIM
        No no - we have our own business to be
attending to

ELFIE
        Excuse me sir, but were you ever a captain of
        a ship you look like you could have been

WAITER
        Me?

ELFIE
        Yeah, you have that look about you

WAITER
     No, I've done many jobs - lowly jobs in the
     city but I have never been even remotely close
     to being a captain of anything

RAZIM
     Okay okay, enough - ELfie please eat -
     thank you, we'll call you back if we need
     you

ELFIE
     Why would she call us that, such a strange
     thing to call some friends -

RAZIM
     We can not use absolutely anything she said -
     it made no sense

ELFIE
     It made a little bit of sense

RAZIM
     Which part Elfie

ELFIE
     Parts

RAZIM
     No one is making any sense these days.
     Not one person.

ELFIE
     I thought she was being - um, let's say

RAZIM
     There was no plot! And the man in the
     forest! What the heck Elfie! And I've just
     lost my job! Nothing makes any sense!

ELFIE
     Don't worry , we've been down worse roads -
     surely this is something we can handle!

RAZIM
where do we go from here?

ELFIE
You know what I've been thinking of - isn't it
funny how performers tend to die on stage like
Tommy Cooper

RAZIM
Gosh, everyone is just giving us their
problems. Please Elfie. You're always
chattering I just want to sit here - you see me
sitting here and trying to think like a smart
man does - just allow me the simple pleasure of
life

ELFIE
So when I was in drama school I was about 20
or so something around there and I thought you know
what!? I'm gonna go into youth theater because
that's where the fun is then I found gay theaters
and now that's fun, forget the posh they're so
boring with their drugs and money and culture nah
boring give me a guy club any day or night and 4
cabarets! I just love the idea really of gay clubs,
they make the effort they do, in their clothes and
their performances kill me and squash all my toes
if I get caught in a business suit ! Also, vintage
China bores me, I had this table you know lovely
table really and I used to tell people come to my
club,it was really just my living room, with a
table on Fridays so the next Friday night we all
dressed up and everyone had to bring their own
drinks and music from their youth the good hits!
That's what we played! To this day those were the
best nights I ever had. I won a raffle too one
night they put the lights on me I got a bottle of
booze let me tell you about that! Now that was a
good memory you got any of those? You know, Ian
Wright did the thing on the telly now he's got a

production company

RAZIM
     Shut up Elfie I can't - I can not deal with
     this - you just - we are looking for
     something right - nothing you say is going to
     lead us there! You need to think like a
     business man, you need to think like an
     economist - weigh the pros and cons of every
     decision you make, you need to do this or
     you're going to end up nowhere in every
     single activity - evaluate, okay? Listen to
     what I'm saying these are big words, I know
     you can get them evaluate, determine and
     execute!

ELFIE
     So there I am dancing having the time of my
     life and you know who comes over... Harvey..
     can you believe it! - puts his briefcase down
     and starts to sing da da da, and I couldn't
     stop laughing and then to make it worse he goes
     picky do dee and that's the end of it and I'm
     sitting there cracking up so I start playing
     the piano to make it look like I'm a part of
     this fiasco right and Harvey always used to ask
     me how's your sister and I never told him I
     knew! I can't say what I knew but I knew and he
     would say to me how's your sister but I never
     told him the romance I knew - I knew but he
     didn't know I knew! And I still know!

RAZIM
     Listen Elfie, you should pay more attention to
your decision making skills. You had a great youth,
so did we all - okay but now is the time you should
really start to understand big words, giant concepts
and vital outlines that I will present to you that
will completely change your perspective on things.
Also,don't mix morals with goodness, you want to be

good - be good! But that doesn't make you moral?

ELFIE
     How so?

RAZIM
     Because a person of integrity, anyone can do
     good - but not be good - a person of morals,
     well they are just

ELFIE
     How many carrots can you eat

RAZIM
     I hate carrots

 THEY EXIT THE TAVERN AND INTO THE NEARBY PARK

ELFIE
     I saw you eat one the other day

RAZIM
     I didn't like it - it was too crunchy

PAINTER
     Is it here, or there? Should I go here or no -
     no - I should go there! No, not there, here!
     Yes here! No, no not here, yes here! No,
     definitely over there - or shall I - no here
     definitely.

RAZIM
     What on earth do you think he is doing?
     Someone has lost it for sure

ELFIE
     Excuse me sir, you look like you are lost. Are
you?

PAINTER
     No, no - I'm just searching

ELFIE
     Searching for what?

PAINTER
     A moment, I'm searching for a moment

RAZIM
     Here we go again, a moment. How are we finding
     all of these people

PAINTER
Yes, a moment, they are all around us everyone
has them but not everyone can appreciate them
because they come and go so quickly! So fast,
so very fast   indeed - I'm a painter, a
discoverer of beauty - a pioneer of the visual
representation of craft - a   moment for me is
what I sketch - you may laugh! It's okay, most
do, chase me away and call me mad. But I will
still be me. It's who I am.

RAZIM
     Elfie, let me tell you something - all artists
     are like this, you'll soon learn in your life
     you have to be reasonable with them and
     approach with care or you'll send them on an
     emotional hurricane. You gotta talk to them on
     their level. Alright here's what I'm going to
     say. (very proudly) Sir, I also find the colour
     and the light something to behold it is
     majestic in its own right - the art of
     expression ! (

ELFIE
     Wow Razim that was beautiful! I never
     thought you could say such a thing

RAZIM
     (pumping himself up) I'm quite educated
Elfie, just listen - where was I, now you see we
are two men - friends - you see - we are searching
for a melody perhaps you've heard of a melody in
these streets

PAINTER
     A melody you seek?

RAZIM
     Yes, a melody we must find, yes indeed. I
     know it sounds crazy but it's -

ELFIE
     A man in the forest told us about it

RAZIM
     Shh Elfie,

PAINTER
     Music, another form of human expression (begins
     humming a tune similar to SHOSHANA)

RAZIM
     Yes yes - all that, indeed. Do you know where
     to find this melody?

PAINTER
     Look at this light! I think I shall

paint it!

RAZIM
     Oh god (puts hands to his face in
despair)

ELFIE
     But what are you doing you're not actually
painting

PAINTER
     No, in fact I like to let the paint do the
     painting - it's kinda like nature - that's
     what I like to do, it's my style!

RAZIM
     (mocking) He has a style, oh god. Elfie
     is this fortune worth it!

PAINTER
     I've kept a reservoir inside of me. Probably
     because I'm unsettled, always unsettled. Always
     moving, never still. A complete nomad, almost
     unable to stay still or in one place for a long
     time.

RAZIM
     Men used to write articles of me and I used to
     go to the BIG institute, I used to call the big
     man who showed me of riches and pleasure. I
     used to be always on the list with other
     pretentious men. Playing golf with sunglasses
     and overpriced shoes! And now I'm here -

PAINTER
     You can only go for so long before the fatigue
     hits you like a train. I went for along time
     with very little, minimum really. I won't
     exaggerate too much, but because of the mayhem
     of a house built by nefarious creatures. The
     problem is I get down, I get very down and I
     can't get back up. I get so far down I can't
     even see up - it's painful and unwelcoming.
     I'm like a poet that doesn't want to be a poet,
     I'm a poet that didn't want to grow old, I'm a
     poet that knows how to write like a child. Who
     ignores debates and chews on art in the mind,
     deflects adulthood, I'm a poet that's a child,
     just a kid really pretending. All I seek in
     life, if someone were to ask me - would be
     inspiration all around - people whom I could
     share with! I suppose, a community of people
     who all shared the same awe in abstract thought
     as I do.

                    I wish I could help you with your song.

ELFIE
             I believe you have. It's what you seek we
             need to tell the man of stories.

PAINTER
             That sounds wonderful, but anyway okay. I
             hope my words were useful (hums)

RAZIM
             Absolutely good luck with everything - come on
             Elfie we gotta keep going.

ELFIE
             Thank you again. We would love to see your
             painting when you finish!

PAINTER
             Sure, anytime - I'm always walking around
             you can find me. (humming loudly and
             singing as he walks away)

RAZIM
             Painters Elfie, they are all the same -
             artists. Abstract. Totally abstract. More
             like high on grass. Let's get this over with.

   ELFIE AND RAZIM ARE WALLKING THROUGH THE STREETS

ELFIE
             Sushi started out as street food

RAZIM
             How do you know that

ELFIE
             I read

RAZIM
     How much

ELFIE
     22 books a month

RAZIM
     No, you don't

ELFIE
     Yeah, pretty much

RAZIM
     No way. That's impossible

ELFIE
     I   do.   (Non   chalantly)   You   think   I'm   so
unsopharted -   unsuficated - unsuccient - un so
fist icarted ? -   unsoooophisticated - Well - But
everyday before I go   to bed I have a bottle of
wine, usually red almost   always red, in fact it
must be red. Not really everyday but a lot of the
time, maybe like a couple of times a year. I don't
know how to drink wine or what smell it's suppose
to have but I always get tired when I drink it.
Look, your brain, look I know this is chemistry but
your brain gets sleepy right -   with wine but some
people they become superwoman or superman and they
become alcoholics, Not me, well. .   okay yeah I get
a little happy but then by the 7th or 8th drink,
yeah I get a little tired, a father once said to me
, children must learn early on what they want -
what was I saying

RAZIM
     How you're so smart

ELFIE
     Right, that I am.

RAZIM
     Look let's go.

ELFIE
      There's a man over there, let's ask him
      what he seeks.

RAZIM
      What an odd game we're playing.

ELFIE
      Sir, sir - we are on a mission to find what
      it is that men seek. Would you mind
      telling us a story.

NOMAD
      Me? I'm just a man on a bench

RAZIM
      Perfect, ordinary man on a bench.

NOMAD
      I have never heard of anyone wanting a story
      in the streets before

ELFIE
      It's like a game we're playing

RAZIM
      We're just curious friends you see

NOMAD
      I think I have many stories.

RAZIM
      We just want to hear something - it can be
anything really at this point the bar is very low

NOMAD
      So you have asked other people?

ELFIE
    We're collecting them

RAZIM
    Some people just blabber on, but yes we are
    asking people - not really sure if we are
    getting anywhere

ELFIE
    True, some of the answers have been hard to
    understand. But I believe in you! You can
    tell us something right!?

 NOMAD
      I could tell you something, sure - not sure
 if it's going to be what you want to hear or not

RAZIM
    Just go on with it

NOMAD
    Let me see… (thinking) okay, let me tell you a
    story of a girl who cared only about herself,
    who made problems - obstacles and enemies
    across all nations. Who hated work, but loved
    money. Stole for bread and shed no tears, who
    imagined herself in glory and fame - yet walked
    in worn torn shoes. Everyday she spread rumours
    in the village proudly saying 'one day I will
    be great! I will be famous, I will be someone!
    Someone amazing! And you all will remember me!
    From bar to bar, meeting and dining with the
    town's misfits. Everyday a new story, an
    imagined life - a never coming glory. The fool
    is one who wanders, who never builds - who
    always grazes off someone else's plate. The
    fool is the nomad, and never glad in a home.
    For ten years I was one - for ten years I
    never built a home. I only wandered. I spent
    ten years a nomad, for ten years I never had a

home. For ten years I roamed the world never
ceasing, packing my belongings and leaving -
eating from pity. For ten years I did this. I
know what it's like to be a nomad, vulnerable
in another language and always in another
man's home. There is something fun and even
exhilarating about moving from one culture to
the next, from going here to there always open
and never having commitments but to tomorrow's
new horizon. It's exciting, travelling. It's
by no means a boring sport, nor dull activity!
Nor does it keep you bland or dreary as an
 individual! Or stale companion at dinner
parties. You'll always have a story to tell,
and you even read the news with more of an
interest. For me, I spent too long a nomad,
that I forgot how to have a home. I can't sit
still anymore, I can't live in one place. I
fall in love, and I can't stay! I taught myself
never to stay. Everyone wants a home, even the
nomad. Some find it in their work - I can't
find it. Always on my tongue, on every
whisper, for me a small prayer: keep the nomad
safe and through distant land's - tales and
stories a head already moving on to tomorrow's
new land.

RAZIM
        Thank you for your time, I sincerely appreciate
 it we don't want to take up to much of your time -

NOMAD
        I like telling stories (hums) -

come back anytime.

ELFIE
        I certainly will!

RAZIM
        We're on a mission, and we really must be

                going. Let's go Elfie, time is ticking!

ELFIE
     It was really nice to meet you.

NOMAD
     You as well. (sings a little song)

RAZIM
     What a waste of time that was!

ELFIE
     It wasn't a waste of time

RAZIM
     Totally was! Come on let's get a few more
     people and hope they give us some better
     answers. This is ridiculous.

ELFIE
     I think some of them are quite...
     interesting. Definitely, something like
     interesting would be the word.

RAZIM
     Her - let's try that girl. Go on and ask, I'm
     getting tired.

ELFIE
     Hello, we understand this is a bit strange to
     ask - but we are men who seek stories to
     find what it is that people in their hearts
     seek after, what gives their life, meaning I
     suppose.

GIRL
     How interesting! Do you work for

someone

RAZIM
     No, we're just -

ELFIE
     Playing a game, sorta

RAZIM
     We are just curious what it is people will say

to us.

ELFIE
     Can you tell us a story please

GIRL
     I would love to! Let's see. How to begin? I hope
     this is good for you. (pauses) A few years
     ago, I gave my heart away, on a soft and misty
     day to a man I thought I knew - I gave my
     heart away when I knew it was wrong and even
     though I had spent many years protecting and
     guarding it - watering my frail heart I gave it
     away at the drop of a hat! Just like that -
     when I thought I knew better, when my feet
     said let's go here and my mind said - I'm a
     bit drunk with happiness let's be the fool -
     try it out - what is it like to live like one!
     And just like that! I gave it away! It was
     rather easy, and I thought - maybe it should be
     more challenging - but it turns out the hard
     part comes after. Winter comes, the sun says
     you have enjoyed too much! You will know life
     with regret. I should've been smarter, wiser -
     more mature, say I. We all make these foolish
     decisions, so I decided - to pick myself up.

ELFIE
     May I ask why you sit in the shadows and not
     in the light?

GIRL
     Because I have a disease that took all of my
     hair - I have no more left. I cannot even bare
     to look at myself in the mirror it has taken
     me a long time to get used to myself.

RAZIM
        May we ask you - what is it that you seek in
life?

GIRL
        I suppose I would like affection, but without
        thinking about my looks without having to curl
        in my thoughts

ELFIE
        Let me tell you something! (changes to a bit
        more lighter tone) If my wife had a bit less
        hair! What a relief! She has so much hair
        sometimes I can't even find her!

GIRL
        Oh how funny

ELFIE
        Don't tell her I told you this

GIRL
        I would never!

RAZIM
        God, why do you do this

ELFIE
        But if they were giving gold medals to
        people with hair! My god! She would win
        the gold! I tell her! Woman you're getting
        hairier by the year! And I'm balding ! Can
        you believe it!

GIRL
        (laughing)

ELFIE
        But I love her all the same. I tell her, when I
        bite a peach I think of you - when I see an
        apple pie I think of you - when I shiver in
        the night I look for you - when I make my
        morning coffee I always think of her.

GIRL
     How sweet (hums as she sits)

RAZIM
     Thank you for sharing - we don't want to take
  up to much of your time. It was kind of you to
                       share.

RAZIM
     I'm going to visit Louisa

ELFIE
     Good, should be nice. I'll be here when you

get back.

RAZIM
     Shouldn't be but a couple hours.

ELFIE
     Take your time, I'll go home too.

RAZIM
     Let's agree to meet here in an hour more

or less.

ELFIE
     Perfect.

                              ENTER LOUISA'S HOUSE

RAZIM
     Get yourself undressed, do it yourself - get
        yourself undressed. Don't feel pressured

LOUISA
        Let me be your rose

RAZIM
        Just get yourself undressed

LOUISA
          Use your words kindly

RAZIM
          Come on now don't make a mess. Let's
          misbehave, let me do the talking.

LOUISA
          Talk to me kindly, talk to me warmly. Write

me a poem

RAZIM
          I don't have time for that

LOUISA
          Write me a sonnet

RAZIM
          I don't have time

LOUISA
          Give me some of your time

RAZIM
          I can't, there's too much to do in this world
          - too many people to meet - too many things
          to do - like I said, I can't

LOUISA
          Brush my hair

RAZIM
          Boring

LOUISA
          Place your hand on my neck

RAZIM
          Would you stop

LOUISA
          Lay down with me

RAZIM
          Already did

LOUISA
        Tell me you care for me

RAZIM
        Do I?

LOUISA
        I wish you cared for me the way I care for
        you - the way I wait for you - the way I love
        you - the way I keep you warm - I wish you
        cared for me, the way Chopin cared for his
        melodies -

RAZIM
        Silly melodies, silly words - people always
        want something silly - women, friends, family
        - silly things they all want. I don't have
        time for simple games, for trivial nonsense,
        for things that make no sense! Games and
        riddles, not for me. I'm a man chisled to be of
        reason. Math and Science, men of philosophy -
        would scoff at such a request. I have to go.
        Now where is that fool, I need to chase a song
        from some man in the forest.

ACT THREE

IN THE STREET ELFIE AND RAZIM CONTINUE

RAZIM
Come on Elfie, let's get back to this nonsense

ELFIE
I find it exhilarting! I wish I had done it
before!

RAZIM
Asking people for a story? You have to work you
know

ELFIE
It doesn't take that much time, and most
people are very happy to be asked!

RAZIM
It's true, but what value comes of it?

ELFIE
A different perspective? Another human's
vision of the life we all are living! It's fun!

RAZIM
When I get my fortune Elfie, listen I am going
to build me a big house and no one apart from those
I allow in will come to me! It will be great!

ELFIE
You know I knew a man who went to prison in
Russia for 8 straight months! Only got out
because of a last minute deal with India,
somehow he got in the mix - you know what he
said after he got out - said, if I had been a

            man of importance I would probably be still
            there . Something to think about!

JIM
       You nasty fool!

ELFIE
       Excuse me sir, but we are looking for

a melody

JIM
       Glorious! What an exciting expedition!

ELFIE
       Sir could you possibly help us?

JIM
       I am just an old man you see - an old man like me
            I'm practically extinct!

RAZIM
       Sir, would you mind telling us - something
that may seem to upset you but you see we believe
the melody has something to do with what
individuals seek - their purpose if you will?
What is it that you seek?

JIM
       Seek? Odd, well - I can tell you about me and I
            have to tell you young ones, I love saying
            this, I have to tell you that I do love
            talking! So I'm more than happy to share with
            you. You see, I am looking to get my visa to
            Vietnam. An old man, I stopped believing in
            love with a woman. Yet I fell in love with a
            girl, you sure wouldn't believe - when I was
            younger, we moved to South Africa, it was
            incredibly awful - insufferable, I hated every
            minute of it you see - I had a child

YOUNG MAN
            Old man! You want a smoke!?

JIM
    This young fool is always bothering me here -
    you   know my name is Jim! Call me by such!

YOUNG MAN
    You want a joint or what, Jam?

JIM
    Jim. It's Jim. You can't ever just leave, can
    you? This boy, all he does is smoke his lungs
    up like he's some furnace - when I was your
    age I was dancing I was partying, I was not
    stealing like you!

YOUNG MAN
    I know you are a fucking old man - nah , let
    me tell you fucking something, you ain't
    fucking worth it! You're just an old man - yo
    - I'm from guess - guess where I'm from and
    I'll tell you what I seek!

JIM
    He's from Romania, and the only word he knows is
    fuck and he steals from everyone. Watch your
                    pockets.

YOUNG MAN
    And what the fuck do you think I seek eh?
    Jam?! Old man!

JIM
    Probably something that rhymes with nancy

YOUNG MAN
    Nancy? What - haha whatever. Yah know me too
    fucking well old man! Don't forget about the
    money eh! No chicks without the dough!

JIM
        This kid annoys me to no end. Is it nancy, or
        was it something else

RAZIM
        Please Jim continue - what is it that you seek

YOUNG MAN
        Boring! Every man seeks the same thing! Yo, why
        you asking these dumb questions - a man no
        matter rich or poor seeks the same thing! Yo, I
        fucking ain't stupid - I could tell you - nah,
        this ain't worth my time - yo I could tell you
        sex and money that's it! I'm outta here

JIM
        Go, please go - he sits around here all day
        just - uff cussing

ELFIE
        We are looking for a melody, we think that
        everyone has a song within them

JIM
        Oh that's a nice thought

RAZIM
        Please continue with your story

JIM
        Well, I'm about to go to Vietnam

RAZIM
        Have you ever been before?

JIM
        Of course! That's how I met the woman I am going
        to marry! Beautiful woman! She loves me! She's
        about 40 years younger than me - but I'm sure she
                         loves me

ELFIE
        Whoa! I was not expecting that! Are you

        sure she loves you?

RAZIM
    Be nice, what we mean is how do you know it's
love

JIM
    And who are you to tell me what love is or what
    it's supposed to be or look like, love is when
    you seek a person you want to be with, no
    matter where they live or if they are a little
    stinky sometimes or have something in their
    teeth or like to eat soup with a fork! You love
    a person when you see them and you feel a
    snuggle inside of you that feels a bit like
    warm and secure. When you trust them, and want
    them to feel good if not sacrifice your
    comfort for them! Love, oh, I love it - I
    didn't have it in my youth, I had lust - got me
    into trouble and a skeleton of a marriage that
    never had beauty - but love , I will not die
    before I experience it. This girl, she's
    beautiful - what a girl, look I'm in my final
    years of life do you really believe I'm going
    to go like my friends sitting in a nursing
    home while my family that I don't even like
    sits around watching me die! Why would I or
    anyone want that! I am an old man in body but
    in spirit I am 20 years old! I don't want to
    accept and I refuse to accept the dim -
    depressing - morbid end just because everyone
    says well that's it you are old, sit down old
    man, I'm not doing anything wrong - the woman,
    she loves me, she doesn't speak much English,
    but I know her heart is for me! Look she sends
    me a picture of her tits everyday!

ELFIE
    Wow!

RAZIM
        Elfie, be respectful

JIM
        (chuckles) Look this is the house we did it in, I
        took a photo to remember! You've got to
        remember things in a relationship, and god
        knows how much longer my mind is going to be
        working! We had to go to Cambodia for this one
        because I didn't have a visa for Vietnam at
        that time and that's when I knew. I've lived
        everywhere Panama, South Africa, and several
        European countries, people tell me - slow down
        old man! My children are waiting for me to
        die! That's what they are doing, and you know
        it will happen - I know it will happen - and
        if I say - look, Cambodia or Vietnam these
        places make me feel happy - that's what they
        do - then why not die happy! When I was a kid
        I followed everyone's rules - I married, got a
        job, a house, a kid - never cheated - paid all
        the bills - did all the right things! And for
        what! When I lived in Malaysia, I thought to
        myself how easy would it be for me to disappear
        - how easy would it be for no one to know that
        I've found a different life.

YOUNG MAN
        (stealing from someone in the street)

JIM
        Would you stop it! I'm going to report you! So
        anyways, that's what I'm seeking - love. Does
        it help with your song? You know I think I

could do my best at singing a song for you!
Let's make it a jazzy one! If I could sing a
song about me it'd go something like (starts
singing energetically): Life! I said Life! Life
is gold! Life is like a puddle to jump in!
Smile! Make a life! You and me! All together!
Life, I said life! I used to follow the rules,
I was the best at it - said - I am ideal! Spot
-on, approval! Then gave up and said - Life, I
said life! I don't want it bland! Forget about
the age! Let's enjoy it! Legally - of course!
You're only alive once! Like a flower let's
admire! Life! I said life! How's that! What
I'm saying is you alone can make yourself
happy doing what makes you happy no matter
what.

YOUNG MAN
     Yo! That's what I'm saying old man!

JIM
     No no - you are doing illegal things! I am not -
     I'm saying make your self happy doing legal
     good things, consentially and perhaps with a
     woman in Cambodia (chuckles) I'm kidding -
     look I don't know how I am so lucky!

RAZIM
     Thank you for your time

ELFIE
     We have got to get ourselves to Cambodia
     Razim! Sounds amazing!

RAZIM
     I believe we have almost got our melody (begins
putting all the songs together with Elfie - singing
and humming)

ELFIE
     Let's see - we should go to the forest to

find the man.

                    FOREST ROAD OUTSIDE CITY

RAZIM
     Here is the man! Look, we have got so many
     stories, perhaps it is now that you are
                    satisfied!

MAN OF STORIES
     (animated) What gives man life and direction? -
     a simple story ! What made the monuments of
     man? - a story! What creates and gives
     knowledge and narrative insights of human
     condition! What do I love! A story! Tell me a
     story I would love to hear one!

RAZIM
     Come on please - not now , we've done
     everything you've said

ELFIE
     I have a story!

MAN OF STORIES
     Tell me!

ELFIE
     A young salesman and a restaurant chef owner
decide to compete by making soup on a cooking show,
a fantastic show! The salesman has the knowledge to
make soup, but the chef always finds a way to outdo
him and just keeps taking home the prize. Each and
every time! The show, let's say it's in China is
awesome! And let's see… The show is like an unknown
name at best and takes place in xinjin province. The
contestant gives up making a lethal drug for himself
instead of knowing that he can still sell it. The
cook was a man with only one daughter but somehow

managed to buy them both food every day, from his
ingenuity and thriftiness he developed recipes which
were so awesome that people would be queuing for
hours to get some! But he lost the show!

MAN OF STORIES
     Oh, what a turn of events! Is this true?

RAZIM
     it was a story -

MAN OF STORIES
     I love stories!

RAZIM
     We have many stories - from the town - which is
what you asked for

MAN OF STORIES
     Yes, true but I feel that you haven't got
     enough! Sing me the melody you have.

ELFIE
     Begins hummming

MAN OF STORIES
     And where are the instruments? You must
     have the instruments as well! Go back
     and continue

ELFIE
     This is so much fun!

MAN OF STORIES
     How many times have you asked those around
     you what they seek - ! Go, and then you get
     your fortune. A fortune that waits for you.

RAZIM
     I don't even have words for how ridiculous
this is. This fortune better be worth it. Come on

Elfie.

ELFIE
Wahoo! This is so much fun!

                THEY RETURN TO THE CITY

RAZIM
Go to him Elfie, let's do this again and don't
forget to ask for an instrument. We have the music
at least.

ELFIE
Excuse me sir, may we ask you what is it

you seek?

DERIK
Oh me?

RAZIM
Yes, please tell us - it is strange and odd

perhaps even weird thing to ask but please -
please tell us something about yourself

DERIK
I'd love to! In fact, I love telling people
     about myself - I'll tell you about myself
     if that's alright?

ELFIE
That's great

DERIK
I am a man dedicated to innovation and
     invention. You   see, I used to make cakes -
     never was one to actually fit in - went to
     Honduras during my military training at 19 -

did that because, well there was nothing else
for a man to do at that time. Found a woman,
and I promised her my love. I took her to
America where we got a home and two kids popped
out. Then I started working at a bakery which
is where I discovered that what I really love
is innovation. (begins pulling out instruments

out of his bag).

The bakery said they would offer a multimillion

dollar contract for anyone who could build a
container that could be baked at a super high
temperature and then be taken home to eat -
well - I baked so many cakes you wouldn't
believe, the entire garage was just filled
with cakes! Cakes were coming   out of the
windows of our house! of our neighbor's
houses! - of anyone that wanted cake! I never
actually discovered the formula however the
government found out what I was doing because
the bakery was actually offering this test via
the government, a little willy wonka action
sort of but government and - well nevermind -
I never got into fairytales - so who would've
thought the government was using a bakery
under the pretense that this formula was going
to be used for cakes - and who knows maybe
originally it was supposed to be used for
cakes but eventually the government got
involved and when that happens you know the
ending of that story - I know movies which
means I know government. (*sniffs proudly like
he's saying something of extreme importance*)
So there I was with all of these cakes and the
cakes were piling up and they didn't stop and
I'm not getting the formula - then I got the

government at my backdoor wanting to - and get this, hire me ! To discover some secret paint for
government airplanes - something top secret can't really talk about it - and I'm telling them, guys look I've never even went to college - heck I'm just a dumb man at the end of the day- but I'm a man of innovation you see! I told them I went to Hondorus once, what in the world am I doing here in
A government top secret location ! You know what they said, you must know SOMETHING because what you're doing not even our smartest, brightest young men can do! And I said, look - I'm not tooting my own horn here - they absolutely said this - now there I am, making some paint for airplanes to fly under radar or whatever - I'm not really supposed to talk about it - and you know then what I figured out! I found how to make an invisible paint for the foundation of house not to burn down completely in a fire and that's when I said adios to the government and said hola to you know what!? BOXES! Because, then I had this brilliant idea - I said, forget about paint, I'm sick and tired of it - although I make about 10 cakes a week still because I'm still trying to find that formula - anyways, I said, I'm a man of innovation -
practically a modern-day Einstein, a genius if you will - what am I doing fooling around with paint for the government ! I said no way - what I need to be doing is working with boxes! Imagine everything in this world practically comes from a distributor and what do they need - everyone needs BOXES! Cardboard - plain, simple brown boxes! Let me tell you what - when this idea came to me I quit my top secret

                job painting for the government - almost on
                the exact day! I said, it's always been boxes!
                Now is that destiny or what?! Here, have some
                cake !

ELFIE
        Wow - Thank you!

RAZIM
        Very kind of you.

    DERIK
                I have this violin and this flute, take
          them - as something to say thank you for
                    listening to my story.

RAZIM
        I'll take that.

ELFIE
        Thank you so much sir!

                    EXIT WALKING THROUGH THE STREETS

ELFIE
        Razim, are you okay? You don't look

so well.

RAZIM
        Just a cough. Let me be

ELFIE
        Okay. What are we going to do about

the melody?

RAZIM
        How will I find my fortune!

ELFIE
        Is that all you think about? Money? Fortune?

RAZIM
        How can you not in this world! How can anyone
        not - it's impossible to live without it -

Elfie, you wouldn't understand because you
just don't care do you, you only care about
your emotions and of feeling good. Let me tell
you what makes me feel good, wealth - security
in finances - okay, call me greedy but that's
what it is - okay and we have go to find this
fortune at whatever costs! Let's go back to the
Man of Stories - I've had enough of this.

THEY FIND THE MAN OF STORIES IN THE OUTSKIRTS OF
                                        THE TOWN

MAN OF STORIES
     So I ask you again, what is it that

you seek?

ELFIE
     Razim, are you listening?

RAZIM
     Where is it? Where is my fortune! I can't live
     like this anymore - outcast, broken to the
     pulp of always seeking but never finding

MAN OF STORIES
     Time will bring to you what your heart
     desires - or ashes they will be

RAZIM
     No, I want it now, where is my fortune

ELFIE
     It's in the community isn't it - that we've
built?

RAZIM
     No, you asked - you promised - a melody we
     bring a fortune you deliver. Here's the
     melody (humming) and here's the violin and the
     flute.

MAN OF STORIES
     (inspecting, sinister and gleefully) One last
     thing I say to you - your fortune lies in a
     small box with a lock in the sea - it will come
     to the shore and to it you must sing the
     harmony to the song I gave you from under the
     rock, you get the song is a bit like a key for
     you today. Only today, no other day. The song
     you sing will open the box. I will give you no
     warning, nor threats nor speak to you again.
     Neither you to me - this is my parting gift
     you see, the song I give to you. Open the box
     if you wish or sing a happy song to your
     grave.

RAZIM
     No more games, no more word plays - I
     want my fortune!

ELFIE
     Razim, calm down

RAZIM
     I am hungry Elfie, (angrily) with a hunger like
     a beast - like one that can only be satisfied
     through fierce action! I am going to the sea!

                    RAZIM LEAVES ANGRILY TOWARDS SEA

MAN OF STORIES
     And you?

ELFIE
     I am worried about this fortune, with the
way you have told us - something isn't right

about it

MAN OF STORIES
     And what worries you

ELFIE
     Perhaps I can't say

MAN OF STORIES
     What is it that you seek?

ELFIE
     It's hard to say - I don't seek much, nor
     fortune everyday. I suppose it would be nice
     to have more things, the comfort of a nice
     home. The richness of a life with enough to
     share with friends. I suppose what I really
     want is just to lie my head in serenity and
     fill my days with companionship let the hours
     pass in sweet folded intention to lead forward
     a good life. Simple. But good. Hard and
     difficult at times we all know to be true such
     a life we all know but above all to seek good.
     A good day. A good laugh. A good meal. A good
     hug. A good life well lived - the only one we
     have.

MAN OF STORIES
     If I were wise - I would tell you to seek
     what's in your heart already put. If I cared
     for you, I might even tell you that greed is
     like a curse. But I think you already know it
     - and as an observer of man I wish to see only
     your reaction and your purpose.

ELFIE
     I also have seen in my life cruel men who
     believed in their riches to save them. Unhappy
     lives they made for themselves. The poison it
     gave to the fair ladies in their lives.

MAN OF STORIES
     Memories are great teachers. The fateful
     shadow that follows your friend, his lust for
     sad songs on the shore, played by his own
     forceful mind is such an unlucky fool

ELFIE
     He has gone through much brutality in his life

MAN OF STORIES
     So have many. And I believe so have you. You
     grew up together right?

ELFIE
     We did.

MAN OF STORIES
     And yet your heart is pure

ELFIE
     Well, pure to an extent

MAN OF STORIES
     You do not climb over men for status, your
     pride has not overtaken you - you speak jolly
     at times but you can be incredibly reasonable
     as well.

ELFIE
     I just don't take things too seriously. Maybe
     I'm a fool

MAN OF STORIES
     Maybe you are. Or maybe you are good

ELFIE
     I want to be

MAN OF STORIES
     Then be good - don't chase the fortune he
     seeks.

ELFIE
     And Razim? What will happen to him

MAN OF STORIES
     It is his story, not yours.

ELFIE
     But I care for him

MAN OF STORIES
     And he is the writer of his own

                         RAZIM WALKING TOWARDS THE SEA

RAZIM
     (*hunched, angry and mumbling*) Creepy man in the
woods what a life he lives, wanting to observe the
acts of man… Tremble! Little insects on earth! God
has taken his blessing for himself! Blessing and
gold for the one who slaves man never to see equal
with diety - blindness for all who try. To sing a
bloody song for a treasure, what a melody full of
nonsense. Incredible the hearts of fools from whom I
will reap and in glory reveal my power over all.
Where is that treasure - the box to which I must
sing into - what a ridiculous strategy for someone
to come up with. What a pest men are. I see the box,
come to me my treasure! My fortune! Make my troubles
at ease and tend to me like a mother to a child as
you mend all my woes, dear Fortune! Take sorrow from
me and lend me a hand in life, dear Fortune I have
struggled in life - and you, you will release me
from my bondage! Come to me - humm, mmm, mm - was
it like this? Mmmm mm the melody? Is this it? Is it
this easy? Mm, mmmm mmmm - mmmmmm! Louder if I must
so that Fortune will be kind! Mmmm, mmm mm, embrace
me my Fortune! Mmmm mmmmm mmmm! Heal me Fortune!
Mmmmm mmm, yes it's opening! Yes yes yes! Give me!

Give it to me! mmmmm, mmm , mmm the song from under
the rock from the fool in the forest! Mmmm, mmm
mmm!!! I'm rich! Ha! I'm rich - my fortune to thine
be forever mine - my beloved - my divine! Girls we
will have, houses we will have, a great future I
will have! Because I have attained it! I have made
it! I have succeeded in fortune I shall lead a great
and wonderful life!

ACT FOUR

SEVERAL YEARS LATER IN A ROOM IN A HOUSE ELFIE AND
                                            RAZIM

RAZIM
     Elfie look! I have 12 pairs of suits! I have
jewels, women - I have it all! Can you believe!
All mine!

ELFIE
     Razim! You have really done it

 RAZIM
     Don't be jealous Elfie, I know you could have
been happy too like me if you had only come with me
that day to the sea. You really made a poor choice,
  whatever that man said to you - you should never
                 have listened!

ELFIE
     True, but I am happy

RAZIM
     Do you have expensive grapes? No - do you have
a different woman for your bed - no - only the
same! Boring. Do you have what all men want! A
palace in God's name! No! You don't - Elfie, I'll
help you out really - but you should look at me
now! I have friends now Elfie, they are important!
Well connected, business men and politicians who
care about me! It's fantastic!

ELFIE
     What will you do about that cough?

RAZIM
     I will buy medicine - what will you do
     about your life?

ELFIE
     I will, I suppose enjoy it

RAZIM
     From a lower standard no? Look, if you want
     I'll invite you to my expensive dinners - no,
     actually I don't like to mix friend groups.
     In fact, I would be embarrassed if they saw
     you.

ELFIE
     That's okay , I can't imagine I would -

RAZIM
     I've met important people now - Kings I've
     shaken hands with! Can you believe it! Prime
     ministers, they want to see the man of
     fortune! Tell the silly man in the forest!

ELFIE
     I suppose it is good we went for the walk after
all

RAZIM
     You know what Elfie, I tell you the truth - it
     truly is!

ELFIE
     Perhaps we could go again one day, for a walk

RAZIM
     I don't have the time for that Elfie and you
     know it. I need to be with successful
     financial savvy important and good looking
     people. I can't be asking them to go for a
     walk with you and me, I have to keep my image!
     You wouldn't understand. If I introduce my

ELFIE
    friends to you, gosh what a beast they would
    think I am! And to ask them for a walk! They
    have so many better things to do! Elfie, why
    are you here!

ELFIE
    I wish I had better news for you. Louisa is
    suffering, from a terrible disease that has
    created the worst -

RAZIM
    Stop, I'll buy her some medicine, she'll be
    fine.   I'll bring her the best doctor's
    with the fortune   I've made I can do it
    all!

ELFIE
    It's quite serious Razim, please listen to
    these few words I give

RAZIM
    Palace and dine! How great I'm living Elfie!
You really messed this up I have the most expensive
suits   - the best shoes - all I could ever want for
me to enjoy! You must go now because I'm having an
expensive dinner tonight with my important friends.

ELFIE
    I wish there was something I could say to you,
    I wish there were something I could do for you
    - something to save you - something to help
    you. Let me play you a song!

RAZIM
    Elfie, I'm fine - you're so sensitive, I
    forgot. Stop trying to play me songs -
    stop with the silly charades. I don't
    want to hear. Look, you are my friend
    too okay? Now please run

ELFIE
    If I could help you - I would have.

RAZIM
     I'm okay! I have fortune!

ELFIE
     Your figure is becoming unfriendly

RAZIM
     I've never looked so good

ELFIE
     Your hands are becoming more callous

RAZIM
     I'm not moisturising

ELFIE
     Your skin is becoming more pale

RAZIM
     You know, I haven't been in the sun

ELFIE
     And your soul is in pain

RAZIM
     It's long dead Elfie, you know that.

ELFIE
     May your health improve

RAZIM
     If I have an opening in my schedule Elfie I'll
     try to schedule you in but you live so far
     really - so look I'm trying

ELFIE
     Just remember the stories of men, and of
     those who sought greed and pride

RAZIM
     The time is running! My patience

is ending

ELFIE
     I'm leaving.

3 WEEKS LATER

RAZIM
Oh a letter! Oh dear. Louisa has passed. I
almost forgot about her. Poor thing. I
will go to her funeral.

AT THE FUNERAL

ELFIE
She was in a lot of pain when it happened.

RAZIM
It's unfortunate. But these things happen.

ELFIE
Your back - it's more hunched

RAZIM
I haven't been exercising

ELFIE
Your hair - it's coarse

RAZIM
The water

ELFIE
You're changing

RAZIM
I'm getting old Elfie.

ELFIE
But you are really changing.

SPEAKER
We are gathered here today, to mark the passing
of a woman who lived here among us. Her life
was short, but filled with goodness. She lived
alone, but was loved by many. A greedy god
desired her, couldn't stand to not have her in

his courts. It is a blessing to know and to
live with the consultation that she is with the
deity - the one and only who truly cares for
her. A better place, some may say - I would
even imagine if I could she is sitting
somewhere smiling under Elohim's gaze, no need
- nor requirement or responsibilities of man,
nor worry nor despair - because like in
Elohim's embrace - like a father to a child,
in holiness she's surrounded in a place so far
we can not imagine here on earth. Lambs
uncovered we are, by the weight of suffering
we live, like a man at a sea on a cloudy and
tormentous life with seas and waves, cliffs in
the distance -

ELFIE
     Where is this going?

SPEAKER
     Holy guidance led her to peaceful waters
     far from what Earth has to offer.

RAZIM
     That was a bit unusual

ELFIE
     You should've come earlier.

RAZIM
     Come by later this evening, I want to talk with
you.

ELFIE
     Your teeth - they are more yellow - and your
     breath it smells terrible

RAZIM
     Parties Elfie, I've been lacking in grooming
     what can I say.

ELFIE
I'll be back later.

MAN OF STORIES
Little men of little monsters, climbing their
way through the silly hurdles made of other
men, laughing the way they do with pride in
their hearts, shoes made from lack of care,
tenderness far from reach, and a little tiny
life they got spent running for the air. Look
at them, I like to do, spending their days on
aimless paths - tell me of the one I want, the
one who sits on humble thrones and tell me of
the one I like, the one who knows of goodness
in sorrow. Tell me of the stories I like, of
the ones who care for small creatures, the
ones who have a plate to share, the ones who
know of the Samaritan's tale. Tell me of the
one who reflects, on good deeds and lives full
of family and with friends. Tell me where they
go and what they do, tell me a story of the
ones who spin lives made in pursuit of light.
Come here little squirrel, come here little
animals of the forest - let me tell you of the
things in my head. Silly mind that goes from
one thought to another, do you know of the
hearts of men?

IN THE ROOM OF RAZIM'S HOUSE

RAZIM
          I was busy, I was really busy. You don't
          understand, everyone wants me! Everyone wants
          to know the man with a fortune! How will they
          look at me Elfie? How will the world judge me?
          What will they say about the man who chased
          his fortune dry?

ELFIE
          I don't know. I wish I could say.. or do
          something for you - be your friend in this
          moment, give you some glimmer of hope. Let
          me play for you a song!

RAZIM
          I'm all alone Elfie, the men in his suits.
          They are like ruthless beasts gorging on
          whatever they find. I don't want to hear a
          song seriously! For the last time.. Eating
          my cheese and my best meats - preying and
          lying and gnawing on life as if it were their
          own personal slave.

ELFIE
          What is it you want now?

RAZIM
          I am old now

ELFIE
          You're not that old yet! Come on!

RAZIM
          I have my fortune, now what. Even the girls
          they steal from me - take every penny I have,
          drugs to numb myself from this - it is never
          enough Elfie. I need more of it. I need more,
          that man - he needs to give me more - I just
          can't have this - I'm running out of
          patience. Where is he!

ELFIE
    You're going mad

RAZIM
    Let me be

ELFIE
    I'm your friend, let's go for a walk! You
love to walk - I love to walk - remember when
we walked   together - what a time that was!
Right?

RAZIM
    You're like a thorn in me, some nagging little
    thorn - constantly in me, what have you done!
    What do you do with yourself! You could've had
    this life - these possessions, my status but
    you chose to squander, what a fool you are.
    Weak-headed imbecile - I pity you, I really
    do. Just get out. Don't come back - stop
    coming here. Elfie, don't you see - I don't
    want you here.

ELFIE
    The moon is higher to the light, and the wind
is a   little longer, I'll remember. The times and
the words. We'll never believe again and the sun is
a little brighter and the moon is a little dimmer.
I'll remember the childhood, and the words we'll
never believe again. I'll remember the times and
the words. We'll never believe again. A simple
chord I know of one forgotten man, who gave a melody
to a simple fool I know come on my friend let's
sing - of the simple words I play for you - I wish
upon you a crown of gentle air - I give to you a
song I sing to you.

RAZIM
    I forgot how poetic you can be when you want
    to. I wish I were more like you Elfie. Like
    small children we used to be, innocent and

               curious - hopeful in distress, and kind in
               agony in horrendous homes, in violent pasts,
               we both came like survivors from the ashes
               you and me.

ELFIE
               I will not let you go yet my brother, but
               you are beginning to make me wonder if
               the man I once new exists in you still.

RAZIM
               I don't know what to do, it's like a consuming
          shadow all around me. This hour you are man, next a
          god in your certain sphere. Lamb once a brute -
          only men who walk this measured way tis doom I try
          to reason. A pioneer for my own sake tis rotten -
          the pity of eternal man. Come to my dinner this
          evening. I am hosting a feast - many women, many on
          display, my fortune for all to see! You should come
          my friend

ELFIE
               Another dinner!

RAZIM
               With important people! And this time I want to
               introduce them to you - see how I'm changing!
               I'm wanting you to be a part of my life! You
               see! It's a good thing to have a friend I've
               learned! Now I want to give you some of this
               fortune I've made! It's a good thing I'm doing
               Elfie for you! Why don't you appreciate the
               little things! I am like Saul, you are my
               David you see! When you play for me a simple
               song, or when you say one of your silly poems
               - it calms me down!

ELFIE
               What's on your head?

RAZIM
               It's nothing but a scratch

ELFIE
     No, there's something there -

RAZIM
     I said tis nothing but a scratch

ELFIE
     No, there's something there! On your head -
     You're getting small horns on your head
     and transforming into something even more
     unkindly - do you not see the greed
     becoming you?

RAZIM
     This is what happens to an old man! Look at
     what I have! All the suits, I could ever
     wish - all the possessions I never had!

ELFIE
     Greed - is - it's actually becoming you!

RAZIM
     Let it rot me! In a home built of gold -
     silver plates

   ELFIE
        Your teeth are rotting, your hands more
  callous - your humped and your likeness more
                    like a beast

RAZIM
        I don't need you to care for me, I don't care
if you don't care for me, I want you to - I believe
it but   people don't do that here do they, they
pretend ,   sure, put on a good show - Sure but do
they care for me? Do they want me? Do you want me?
Do you care for me? I wish you did, I want you to
but don't it'll   make me stronger, more of a
fortress. I spent my life on a beach hidden by god
for he is a god of wrath, I was taken care of for a
while by the soil. I choked on sorrow like in a fit

of rage. I could not leave. I spent my life on a
bench you see, watching people around me claw their
way towards fortune. I spent my life in a box you
see, something like a deep hatred for humanity fell
over me, with a father whose toxin bled into me -
dear family what did you do to me.

ELFIE
        You are not well! You make little sense, you're
        figure more and more terrible to look at! You
        should come out of this mess you're making -
        you're not even that old! This fortune is
        rotting you - your life is becoming, like a
        legend to be told of - like one that you pity
        - like one that makes you shudder! Is that
        what you want! Truly! I'm your friend, let me
        help you - if not to only save you from your
        coming end

RAZIM
        Don't test me, rebuke me but don't test me -
despise me but do not test me. What a fool you are
to come for me as if you would, as if you could
defeat the villain in your stories. I used to live
a life of extreme isolation of terrible loneliness
with a wicked mind a solitude no man knows - tell
me what is one more day!

ELFIE
        I will go to the Man of Stories Razim, I will
        ask him what to do

RAZIM
        Just go. Don't come back. Leave me be.

                                        IN THE FOREST

MAN OF STORIES
     They told me, what a man they said to me as
     they laughed in my face! Who would be a
     dishonest crook such as that - not I for I
     know that a crook walks a crooked path not long
     does he before crooked legs has he. A deer and
     a man both have in common one thing the need of
     their senses to bring them to water

ELFIE
     Who are you speaking to?

MAN OF STORIES
     Just - the air I guess

ELFIE
     I see, ahem, I need to save my friend!

MAN OF STORIES
     Am I god, clearly not! A glass of whiskey in
     the right hand, a woman maybe two I thought he
     would perhaps ask for but like the gas
     breathes fire a deep void he meant to fill of
     solitude I did not know the character of man,
     my observation - as one gazes at the moon and
     stars above - working at puzzles over their
     complexities - so do I with men, looking at
     celestial beings as something like a galaxy
     within. Different everyone, one a hermit -
     another a prince of his own space, of his own
     time, family, worth and value

ELFIE
     Can you save him?

MAN OF STORIES
     Longing for the grave, I did not expect him to
     be so earnest, the doors of awakening like the
     morning tide prove me to show

ELFIE
     Please, speak to me in words I can
     understand and release him from whatever
     spell or witchcraft you have placed him
     under

MAN OF STORIES
     This isn't your story - this is his. There once
     was a man who had a strong mind, incredibly
     strong and resilient. Then people began to
     notice his hard work - said, this is a man who
     works hard, does good and noble deeds never
     asks, and always gives - so they began to
     promote him and give him success. Because he
     had never been given an easy day in his life
     all this time he worked and worked, never
     asking for more than his needs even to god he
     said - I will not ask from you. Who would've
     thought, out of all the struggles in his life,
     the success would bring him down. You know
     why? Because someone used to struggle and
     torment, doesn't know what to do in the years
     of peace.

ELFIE
     Can you please just help him

MAN OF STORIES
     It is not my story - it is his. He is the
     writer not you. It is not for us to rewrite.
     Do you remember the melody?

ELFIE
     A beautiful melody it was

MAN OF STORIES
     Do you know what key it was in?

ELFIE
     Perhaps a big one?

MAN OF STORIES
     It was in G Minor - sit on a bench with me,
     calm your mind and listen to the sounds you
     hear around you. A bird, maybe a breeze - and
     remember what you hear. Cross the rapids and
     go back to the city but this time be mindful of
     the noises and avoid the distractions. Enjoy
     the little parts that make your day, the small
     moments of ease and relief, take joy in what
     you have and remember not all suffering is for
     you to fix. Do what you can, be good to your
     family, tell your friend you are here for him -
     but to make your life an avalanche of disaster
     from his decision - a terrible thing indeed.
     Not that I care, what you do, nor who you are
     - I'm just an observer really in all of this.
     But if I could offer some advice. I would say,
     he chose his fate you choose yours Elfie. Do
     you remember the song, I love that song - I am
     making a new one, going to hide it in a tree
     this time, maybe in the river -

ELFIE
     I knew when you were sounding normal it was
     short lived

MAN OF STORIES
     Composing music in my time from the stories
     I hear, keeping me sane in this time.

ELFIE
     It was a beautiful song

MAN OF STORIES
     One of my favorites! A gentle melody wasn't it!

ELFIE
     Really gentle, something like a first kiss.
     Light and gentle.

MAN OF STORIES
     I was inspired by the stream where the animals
     come to drink. Do you know between the cracks
     and cement, holding the power of one and
     finding the strength the rain drops and the
     insects buzz nearby neither the strongest nor
     the most beautiful the small stem holds all but
     one. I see on my walks the perseverance of all
     but one stem in the cracks of the cement.
     That's like goodness in this world. Like you
     Elfie bringing goodness in the world

ELFIE
     I just wish I could give Razim a melody that
     would relieve him from his chaos. He's becoming
     more like a beast than man.

                         IN A ROOM OF RAZIM'S HOUSE

ELFIE
     My god! You are a beast Razim! You are
actually a beast! Your face! Did you scratch it
off?

RAZIM
     Keep me hidden, oh god for the sake of
humanity! Keep me hidden what a terrible mind my
father gave me. Completely crushed, unable to hold
itself - poor thing. I hide it very well, the
monster in my head, keeping it peaceful one word of
gentleness abates it - one word of love soothes it,
put it away - Elfie, this will be the last time you
see me! Never come back ! Do you understand! I will
never be kind to you - I will never want you here!
I am going to lock myself here! I cannot be seen
like this! Promise me never come back here Elfie! I
will hurt you! Leave! Leave and don't come back!

                                        TEN YEARS LATER

CHILD
      Who is that?

MOTHER
        That is the man who found a fortune, he went
        mad and goes around telling people stories
        asking if they want to hear a song. He sits
        alone all day in his big house. His greed made
        him into a beast.

                                        ANOTHER DAY

CHILD
       (sneaks into Razim's dark house)

RAZIM
        (*hears something*) Elfie is that you? Did
        you come back? Are you okay?

CHILD
       No - I just

RAZIM
       I'm sorry, I'm slow to sight and

to move

CHILD
       So it's true, you have become a

beast

RAZIM
       Is Elfie here?

CHILD
       I don't think so

RAZIM
       I miss him

CHILD
      What happened to you?

RAZIM
      Haven't you heard?

CHILD
      I have.

RAZIM
      My story is finished.

CHILD
      It isn't

RAZIM
      I've become the beast in your story

CHILD
      You can still try

RAZIM
      You don't know what I've been through

CHILD
      No, I don't

RAZIM
      Cruel and terrible world of men

CHILD
      I wouldn't know

RAZIM
      Why are you here?

CHILD
      I don't know. I wanted to see for myself.
      If the story was true.

RAZIM
      Well - it's here, I'm here, it's true. It's

all true.

CHILD
      You don't seem mean

RAZIM
    I am

CHILD
    You don't seem scary

RAZIM
    I am!

CHILD
    You seem sad, but you don't

seem scary.

RAZIM
    I suppose, I am

CHILD
    So you go around calling yourself the man of
    stories now right?
RAZIM
    I do

CHILD
    I like stories

RAZIM
    I think everyone does

CHILD
    Have you thought finishing yours

RAZIM
    Mine is finished

CHILD
    But it isn't

RAZIM
    It's done. Finished. This is my fate.

CHILD
    You could still change it though, have
    a happy ending?

RAZIM
    How would I do that?

CHILD
By speaking it, by saying it - maybe? By
telling a story that ends well?

RAZIM
I miss Elfie. You sound like him a little.

CHILD
Did you by any chance ever find out what
Elfie's fortune was?

RAZIM
What?

CHILD
You got your fortune - but did you ever want
to know what his was?

RAZIM
I don't understand

CHILD
Each of you got a fortune remember? What you
want, what you seek - don't you remember?
I've heard the story a thousand times

RAZIM
It was a fortune

CHILD
To each it was a fortune - to each it was
what you seek

RAZIM
What was it that he sought!

CHILD
There's a plate set every night in my house for
you. Come and see one day. We don't live here
in the city, we live more in the country area.
Elfie said you will know where to go. But you
should come one day. I have to go now, they

will know I'm missing.

RAZIM
Mad, I'm mad - I'm a lunatic. I should never
listen to voices. I can barely see. My sight
is gone. My face I've peeled, my hands more
resemble claws, I am a beast never to leave
this palace I made. I cannot feel, I cannot
live in peace! All I want is peace in my mind
now voices in my head. Never a day passes that
my mind doesn't try to jump far from me! But,
what was it that Elfie got? What did he want?
What did he seek that poor fellow. What a life
I envy. What a kind man to me in my horror.
Never left my side till I pushed him out.
Elfie, what was it that you sought? What could
it be! Another song ,another melody? Perhaps
another woman, no he was loyal. A happy life
away from me it must be! The outskirts, hills
and fields - where we grew up - he must be
there. Should I see him? Would he want to see
me? Lonely days locked away, a beast left to
be. One long friend I must see. Before my doom
I must know - what fortune it was he chased.

ELFIE
Come on everyone ! It's dinner time , my
favourite time of day always a meal -

RAZIM
It's Elfie! (*peaking through a window*

from a tree in the distance) I see him!
Would he want to see me?

ELFIE
Everyone together!

MAN OF STORIES
Look who is here , hiding in the forest

RAZIM
You ! You mad man! You watched me destroy
myself for your entertainment!

MAN OF STORIES
A gift you turned to a curse, the curse you
made yourself - the gift I provided for
the stories you collected. I heard you also
call yourself my name

RAZIM
How can you just watch me in my solitude

MAN OF STORIES
There are many tales of suffering in the city,
yours is not the worse. I see many who hurt. I
see the ones in pain, many who walk with
thorns on their back. You are not the only
one.

RAZIM
I am too tired and hard of hearing, slow to
move and miserable to fight with you.

MAN OF STORIES
     Your friend, he always asked of you.

RAZIM
     I tore at my face everyday

MAN OF STORIES
     He always tried

RAZIM
     I never let him near

MAN OF STORIES
     His family cares about you

RAZIM
     I have no one left.

MAN OF STORIES
     You had his loyalty

RAZIM
     And I locked the door

MAN OF STORIES
     It is not finished yet , your story

RAZIM
     What was it that Elfie wanted?

MAN OF STORIES
     A table full of all his friends, a home full of
     health and laughter, quite simple and easy
     really. People respect him for it, come to see
     him for advice. He's done quite well, even I
     thought he was a bit of a fool for a bit, but
     it turned out that he's really quite sensible
     underneath it all.

RAZIM
     He's always been like that. Likes to make
     light of everything.

MAN OF STORIES
     I quite like Elfie

 RAZIM
     Me too - I miss him. I'm glad he's well.
 My one friend, might be the only one I ever
                    had.

MAN OF STORIES
     There's one more thing he asked for

RAZIM
     What's that

MAN OF STORIES
     I think he knew you were headed toward doom in
     some way or fashion, I'm not sure - but he
     knew. The day you went running for your
     fortune we spoke for a bit - I advised him not
     to go with you. The fortune he sought was a
     melody to be your remedy for when you reach
     your end. I believe that must be now. It is his
     song to sing - perhaps he's hidden it under a
     rock, or under a pillow or maybe keeps it in
     his pocket. Maybe he gave it up and sent it
     flying away. I don't know. A remedy for your
     sorrow is what he asked.

 RAZIM
     I can not go to him now

MAN OF STORIES
     What interesting characters you two are! I
     told you! I even myself thought I wouldn't
     tell you - yet here I am telling you - silly
     me! Well, now you know - I told you because
     looking at the scars on your face and your
     beastly figure, it draws sympathy from me.
     But this is all I can do.

RAZIM
     Elfie...

MAN OF STORIES
     You don't have many options now.

RAZIM
     I can't

MAN OF STORIES
     I don't care what you do - I'm just here to
     observe. But if I did care for you, I would
     say you should go to him, he's good at heart.
     His family are warm people, some of my
     favourite to watch on this land. But I am just
     an observer so I cannot say. But maybe, maybe
     you should go to them?

RAZIM
     I will wait till morning to decide

MAN OF STORIES
     Up to you to decide of course but (starts
     screaming) - Elfie! Elfie come out here!
     Elfie! Elfie where are you!

RAZIM
     What are you doing!

MAN OF STORIES
     Just helping the story out!

RAZIM
     I'm not ready!

MAN OF STORIES
     Elfie! We are over here!

ELFIE
     Is someone calling my name? I think I hear
someone calling my name! How exciting! Must be a
friend, or someone who has something good to tell

me! Or a surprise! I love surprises! A surprise
it is!

MAN OF STORIES
      Good luck, I've done all I can do

RAZIM
      No - don't go!

ELFIE
      Hello! Who is there!

RAZIM
      No, no no - I can't do this - he is - not
      going to - understand

ELFIE
      Hello?
RAZIM
      Elfie, it's me!

ELFIE
      Razim!

RAZIM
      Yes

ELFIE
      You came?

RAZIM
      I just -

ELFIE
      Come inside

RAZIM
      I can't I -

ELFIE
      What are you doing here?

RAZIM
      I just - I don't

ELFIE
      I'm glad you are here.

RAZIM
     I don't know what to say to you

ELFIE
     It's okay, you don't have to say

anything

RAZIM
     I pushed you away

ELFIE
     You did

RAZIM
     I was in deep pain and despair

ELFIE
     I kept trying to come in - but the door was
     locked so well - I tried for many years!

RAZIM
     I couldn't let you in, to see what I became

ELFIE
     Come inside - my wife will make you something
     to eat and you can meet my family

RAZIM
     I'm a beast now, I can't - I just don't think
     I can do it

ELFIE
     I have a remedy for you

RAZIM
     I heard

ELFIE
     I keep it in my pocket for the day I

see you again.

RAZIM
     I wish you didn't

ELFIE
     But I did. You're home now. Let me play you a
song

               [ELFIE moves towards a small, old piano
               in the corner of the room. He sits
               down and begins to play a gentle,
               soothing melody. RAZIM slowly moves
               closer, drawn in by the music.]